sashes red and blue

sashes red and blue

by Natalie Savage Carlson

AUTHOR OF *THE TALKING CAT*
AND *WINGS AGAINST THE WIND*

Pictures by **RITA FAVA**

Harper & Brothers, Publishers, New York

J

c.1

sashes red and blue

Copyright © 1956 by Natalie Savage Carlson

Printed in the United States of America

Library of Congress catalog card number: 56–8144

foreword

IN FRENCH CANADA, THE LE BLANCS ARE LIKE SMITHS IN this country. There are so many of them that they have spilled over into New England. And this is fortunate for New England because the LeBlancs are fine people and hard workers. Most of all, they have become good American citizens.

Charles LeBlanc is mayor of his little town in Vermont. Emilie LeBlanc teaches school in Portland. Old Pierre LeBlanc has one of the biggest farms in his part of Maine. They all say that some day baby Baptiste LeBlanc will be President of the United States. And *parbleu*, Antoine LeBlanc is the best millworker in Woonsocket.

But the LeBlancs cannot forget that they came from French Canada and that many of their relatives still live there. Because they want to keep these memories alive for their children as well as themselves, they set a day once a year to meet for a LeBlanc reunion.

They have a big picnic in the park with pork pies and *croquignoles* and all the good things that were first cooked in Canada. Of course there are dozens and dozens of children at the LeBlanc reunion, because French Canadians love children and all children love a *picque-nique*.

After everyone has eaten until he can hardly move and sung "Alouette" until he is almost hoarse, there are still those left who want to talk about things that happened to well-known LeBlancs back in Canada long ago. All the children crowd around, because what is more fun than listening to stories when one can eat cakes while doing it and know there are still more left on the long table?

contents

LUC BOULANGER'S SPOTTED PIG   I

CLAUDE LeBLANC AND THE *FI-FOLLET*   10

SASHES RED AND BLUE   22

LITTLE NICHET'S BABY SISTER   34

THE DANCE OF THE MARIONETTES   44

THE HARD MASTER   53

HOW LITTLE NICHET BECAME
    JEAN-BAPTISTE   65

THE *LUTIN* IN THE BARN   80

THE SHEEP WITH THE WOODEN
    COLLAR   92

sashes red and blue

Luc Boulanger's spotted pig

IT HAS BEEN TEN, MAYBE FIFTEEN, YEARS since anybody has seen the LeBlancs from Charlevoix. That Jean LeBlanc had one fine family. Those children must be grown up now with children of their own.

Jean LeBlanc was very proud of his fourteen children. They were good children and they helped him on the farm. My faith, that man did not have to worry about having extra hands for the plowing and the harvesting. Not with those six strong boys who began with Pierre-Paul and went all the way down to little

Nichet, the nest egg. And Madame LeBlanc did not have to worry about extra hands for the cooking and washing and sewing. Not with those eight strong girls who began with Marie-Louise and went through all the Maries down to Marie-Elaine.

Only trouble Jean had with those children was all the questions they would ask. From big Pierre-Paul down to little Nichet, they were as full of questions as a porcupine of quills.

"Papa, why is it night half of the time and day the other half?"

"Papa, why do horses eat hay? Why don't they eat bread and soup like we do?"

"Papa, how many ants are there in all the world?"

Jean LeBlanc could take care of their questions though. When one of his little LeBlancs asked him something, he would make a wise face. He would say, "If I tell you the answer, you will forget it. But if you find out for yourself, you will always remember."

"But how can I find out why our cows don't have wings like our chickens, Papa?" perhaps one of them would ask. "Do you know?"

"Of course I know," surely answered Jean LeBlanc.

"Now find out for yourself. Then tell me the answer and I will let you know if it is right."

This worked out very well because the children would bother other people with their questions instead of their father. They would go to the neighbors or the people in the village or wait for the meatman to drive around in his four-wheeled wagon.

"Our cows do not have wings because they do not belong to the bird family," little Marie-Elaine told him. "That's what my teacher said."

Little Marie-Elaine never bothered the neighbors or the people in town or the meatman, because she found out that they usually didn't know any more about it than she.

Then Jean LeBlanc made his very wise look.

"Your teacher is right," he said. "She is a smart woman. Of course cows do not belong to the bird family. That is why they have no wings."

So the little LeBlancs knew that their father was smart, too, because he had known the answer all along.

One day when half or maybe a third of the little LeBlancs were helping their father to drive the pigs to the woods to feed on acorns, little Nichet asked, "Papa, why do pigs have curly tails? Why aren't they straight, like the tails of horses and cows and oxen?"

Jean made his very wise look at his littlest child.

"If I tell you the answer, my little nest egg," he said, "you will forget it right away. But if you find out for yourself, you will remember it forever."

So little Nichet tried to find out for himself. First he asked his mother.

"Mamma," he asked, "why do pigs have curly tails?"

But Mamma did not make a wise look at all. She only shrugged her shoulders.

"I know nothing about it," she said. "All I know is that I do not put them up on curl papers every night. Believe your mamma, she has enough to do taking care of fourteen children without spending her time putting up pigs' tails in curl papers. And that brings something to my mind. If you fourteen children are to have supper tonight, I will need some more wood for the stove. Fill the woodbox with kindling for your mamma."

So little Nichet quickly saw that he had asked the wrong person. But he filled the woodbox anyway because he was an obedient little boy.

Next Nichet went to the bedroom where his grandmother was winding wool balls.

"Grandmère," he asked, "why do pigs have curly tails?"

"To make little boys ask their grandmothers foolish questions," said Grandmère. "Now answer me a question. Who is going to help me untangle this wool?"

Nichet could answer that question without opening his small mouth. He looked for loose ends and picked little bunches loose until the wool was ready for balls.

Nichet asked his eight sisters and his five brothers, but they didn't know either. They didn't even care. They all thought that pigs were very uninteresting and that their tails didn't matter at all. Poor little Nichet couldn't ask his teacher because he didn't have a teacher. He was too little to go to school.

Jean LeBlanc took a great interest in little Nichet's search for the right answer. Sometimes he stood by the pigpen in deep thought and watched the pigs and their curly tails. And all the while he made a very wise look on his face as if he and the pigs shared a tight secret.

One evening when Jean LeBlanc was not too busy with farm work, he walked over to visit his neighbor, Luc Boulanger.

"Luc," he said, "you have been farming for a long time and you know more about beasts than I. Why do pigs have curly tails?"

Luc Boulanger snorted through his hairy nose. "Jean LeBlanc," he said, "you ask more foolish questions than your children. That reminds me. My old spotted pig has rooted under the fence again. Will you help me chase him back into the pen?"

Jean LeBlanc was as willing a worker as his little son. He helped Luc look into the slop barrel and under the corncrib and everywhere a curly-tailed pig might take himself.

At last they found Luc Boulanger's old spotted pig eating the fat cabbage weeds at the far corner of the cow pasture.

"*Oinque, oinque,*" said the old spotted pig and he went on eating the fat cabbage weeds. He wanted to stay in the cow pasture. He did not want to return to the pen. If he had wanted to stay in the pen, he wouldn't have rooted his way out in the first place.

"Go! Go!" cried Luc, waving his arms at the pig.
The pig shook his ears out of his eyes and glared
at Luc. Then he went the wrong way. *Zigue-zague*
went the pig. Luc and Jean LeBlanc went *zigue-
zague* and *zague-zigue* after him. The pig didn't run
very fast and the men ran so fast they nearly ran out
of their shoes. But the pig always got away from
them. They chased him through the garden and
around the slop barrel and through the barn.

"We've got him cornered," panted Jean at last. "If
only he would be reasonable, we would have him
back in the pen in no time."

"I have never known a swift ox or a reasonable
pig," said Luc Boulanger. "You will have to open

the gate quickly while I drive this pig into the pen."

Jean sneaked past the pig as if he didn't even see him standing there with his trumpet nose and curly tail.

The man stood by the pigpen with his hand on the gate because if he opened it too soon, the other pigs would get out. Luc headed the spotted pig in the right direction. He waved his arms wildly and yelled things that only a pig would not take as insults. Jean opened the gate just in time. But he was so afraid that the pig would change its unreasonable mind at the last minute that he slammed the gate shut on its curly tail.

"*Oinque, oinque,*" squealed the spotted pig. And when it pulled loose from the gate, all the curl had gone from its tail. It was broken in three places and hung straight as a cow's. But the old pig didn't care because he suddenly discovered that there had been fat cabbage weeds growing in the pigpen all the time.

"*Oinque, oinque,*" said the pig, as if he had wanted to get back in the pen all the time.

Luc thanked Jean and Jean thanked Luc. But neither of them thanked the pig for anything.

When little Nichet came to his father and said, "I give up, Papa. No one knows why pigs have curly tails. Will you tell me?" his father took the little boy in his lap the way he always did when he had a special secret.

A wise look made itself on Jean LeBlanc's face.

"Not all pigs have curly tails, my little nest egg," he said. "Luc Boulanger has a spotted pig whose tail is as straight as your hair."

Little Nichet was astonished at this news from his papa who knew so many things.

"Why does Monsieur Boulanger's pig have a straight tail, Papa," he asked. "Why? Why?"

Jean LeBlanc's look became very, very wise. "Because some stupid fellow slammed a gate shut on its tail," he answered.

Then little Nichet was satisfied that his father knew everything in all the world.

Claude LeBlanc
and the *fi-follet*

*Y*OU REMEMBER THAT CLAUDE LE BLANC WHO lived by Baie St. Paul? There was one brave man. In Baie St. Paul the old heads still remember the time Claude caught the *fi-follet* in a bag. These days not many people know about the *fi-follet*. A tiny fellow he was—no bigger than your thumb. He went about at night, carrying a little lantern. He tried to get mortals to follow his light so he could lead them into bogs or over cliffs.

Everyone by Baie St. Paul, or anywhere else in Canada for that matter, used to fear the *fi-follet*. They stuffed rags into every crack and keyhole to keep him out at night. Because once the *fi-follet* got inside a house, he would grow bigger and *bigger* and BIGGER until he was big as a giant. Then he would break the furniture and the walls and the people. *Cric, crac,* break a back!

Pif! Paf! Pouf! Claude LeBlanc didn't fear lightning, the devil, or the *fi-follet*.

"If that little goblin creeps into my house," said Claude, "by my faith, I will catch him in a paper bag and light my pipe with his lantern."

So everyone in Baie St. Paul rolled his eyes in his own head and hoped in his own heart that if the *fi-follet* did get into any house, by his faith it would be the house of Claude LeBlanc.

For truth, although Claude was a brave man, he had few friends. He cracked his own whip too much and was in the habit of making fun of the fears of his neighbors.

"You, Philippe Besette," said Claude, "I think you are afraid your own dog will bite you. Pif!"

Or, "Why do you take the long road around the woods at night, Charles Piche? Fear you that there is a bear waiting behind every tree? Paf!"

So the people by Baie St. Paul may be forgiven if they even hoped the *fi-follet* might get into Claude LeBlanc's house one night and grow into a giant and crack his back just one little *cric*. Philippe Besette, Claude's neighbor across the wheat field, even hoped the *fi-follet* might give two or three little *crics* to the brave man's back.

But a man who feared neither lightning, the devil, nor the *fi-follet* was not likely to worry about what his neighbors thought.

Claude LeBlanc didn't fear hard work either. He planted his wheat field and watched his crop grow tall and green. At harvesttime he cut his wheat and gathered it into neat piles in the field. What matter that it rained before he could winnow the grain? Rain was only water but Claude LeBlanc was bone and muscle. He turned and spread all the piles of wheat to dry in the new sunshine that followed the rain.

That night Claude went to bed early because he was so tired from the day's work in the wheat field. He closed his heavy eyelids and let out one big groan of weariness and happiness that the hard day was over. He fell fast asleep and began dreaming that he was lifting the heavy pitchforks of wheat again.

Then a noise awakened Claude. It was a scritch, scratch noise. It came from the other side of the wall, the side of the wall that faced on the swamp where so often the people of Baie St. Paul had seen the *fi-follet* beckoning to them with his little light.

Claude's wife heard the scritch, scratch too. Madame Solange attacked her husband as if he were a pan of dough. She pinched him and punched him.

"Wake up! Wake up!" she cried in terror. "The *fi-follet* is trying to get into our house."

"I am already awake," said Claude. "What good does it do me to sleep when I only go back to work turning the wheat?"

"Then do something," cried Madame Solange. "Make the *fi-follet* go away."

"You have already stuffed the keyhole and all the cracks," he reminded her. "What is left for me to do?"

"He will scratch through the wall and get into our house," cried Madame.

"Then you had better pull the rag out of the keyhole so he can get in without making holes in the wall," said Claude LeBlanc. And he turned over and began dreaming again that he was still out in the field lifting the heavy pitchforks of wheat.

But poor Madame did not sleep a wink because she was so frightened lying there and listening to the *fi-follet* scratching to get in.

For three nights, the *fi-follet* scratched and scratched. For three nights, Claude snored and snored and dreamed that he was turning the wheat. For three nights, Madame Solange pinched him and punched him and begged him to do something.

Everyone by Baie St. Paul heard about what was going on nights at Claude LeBlanc's house. Everyone was glad it was that house and not his own.

When Claude went to the village, everyone asked him about the *fi-follet*. Even if they didn't like him, they wanted to know what was going on at his house.

Claude LeBlanc only laughed and rolled his own eyes in his own head. "Pif! Paf! Pouf!" was all he said. He thought that the curious people should make their own excitement.

When he returned from the village, Madame Solange met him at the door. She had a rolling pin in one hand, a poker in the other. Any husband other than Claude LeBlanc would have run away from a wife so armed. But the brave man only pinched her cheek.

"Are you expecting company?" he asked.

"Ha! I can promise you that we will have company before tomorrow morning," promised Madame Solange. "The *fi-follet* has made his way through the wall at last." She showed him a little hole near the floor. "He will surely get us tonight. Oh, Claude, let us move away. Let us go to Baie St. Paul and live in town where the walls are close together."

"Pif! Paf!" said Claude. "I will catch the *fi-follet* in a paper bag. Get me one from the kitchen closet."

Then Madame started a great heaven-help-us-all. She wanted to nail a board over the hole or burn down the house or sleep in the barn with the cows.

"Such nonsense!" said Claude LeBlanc. "I will catch the *fi-follet* in this bag and that will be the end of him."

"It will be the end of us all," cried Madame Solange. "And then what will it matter that you were such a brave man when alive?"

But Claude went on saying "pif," "paf," and "pouf." He carefully laid the paper bag by the hole. He ate his dinner with relish, but Madame did not touch a bite because she felt that it would be her last one.

As night began to lower, Claude began getting ready to receive the company that Madame expected to come through the hole in the wall.

"Put out all the lights," he ordered his wife. "Then stand guard at the dormer window."

"If I die," cried Madame Solange, "I want to die with the lights on."

"The *fi-follet* will not come in the house while the lights are on," he reminded her.

This gave Madame a new thought. "That is it, Claude," she cried happily. "We will leave the candles

burning all night long. Then the *fi-follet* won't come in."

But Claude LeBlanc shook his head.

"Have you no sense of thrift, my wife?" he asked. "Better the *fi-follet* should break us to pieces than waste all our candles."

So Madame blew out the candles. Then all was black as the inside of an oven. She somehow found her way up the steps to the dormer window.

"Tell me when you see the lantern of the *fi-follet*," ordered Claude. "I will get ready with the bag."

Madame waited at the dormer window. She stared out into the black night. She thought about her great-grandmother who had watched at this same window for Indians. She thought of her grandfather who had watched at this same window for the British. She thought of her Aunt Mathilde, who had watched at this same window for the beau who never came. Most of all she thought about herself watching for the *fi-follet*.

Suddenly she put her hand to her mouth to keep a scream inside. For her eyes saw the light of the *fi-follet* flickering across the swamp.

"He's coming, Claude," she cried. "He's coming toward the house."

So Claude put the mouth of the paper bag over the hole in the wall. He waited and waited and waited even longer.

At last there was shrill laughter from a tiny voice and something jumped into the bag.

Claude's big hands twisted it shut.

"I've got him, Solange!" he cried. "I've caught the *fi-follet*! He's a strong one. I will have to hang onto this tight if I want to keep him caught."

All night long, Claude held the bag tightly in his hands. And what a fight that *fi-follet* put up! He shrieked and twisted and jumped about until the man's arms ached from the struggle.

At dawn the *fi-follet* was still trying to get out of the bag. Madame Solange hitched the horse to the buggy and drove her husband and the *fi-follet* to Baie St. Paul. At each farmhouse they stopped long enough to tell the owners that Claude had the *fi-follet* in a bag and was taking him to the store in Baie St. Paul so everyone would know he was telling the truth. Other horses and buggies were soon on the road to town. It was like market day.

At first no one would come into the store with Claude, not even the man who owned it. Finally they grew braver, for even fear can become a dull thing if nothing really happens. They gathered around Claude LeBlanc.

"Bring me that empty glass jar on the shelf," said Claude. "I will drop the *fi-follet* into it so everyone can see him. Put it on the counter here. Now give me plenty of room."

Everyone stepped back so quickly that Claude had all the room he needed. Some even ran outside to make more room.

Claude LeBlanc slipped the mouth of the paper bag over the glass jar and gave the bag a shake. And what should drop into the jar but a little field mouse with a long thin tail. It surprised Claude so much that he knocked the jar on the floor. It broke into two pieces and the little field mouse ran back and forth, back and forth. It didn't grow into a giant and break everything in sight. It just—disappeared into thin air.

But it left Claude trembling with fright.

"Mice!" he cried. "Mice in my wheat field! They will eat all my grains of wheat. After I have worked so hard for the harvest. Now I have mice to fight!"

And he was so frightened and worried that he bought two dozen mousetraps and four cans of rat poison and offered the storekeeper a home for all the kittens his cat might ever have. Then he hurried home to turn the wheat piles all over again.

Claude LeBlanc's neighbors laughed at him. They felt good to see that there was something the brave man feared. It made them like him. So they stopped laughing. They helped him set his traps and put out his poison and turn over his piles of wheat.

They even decided that Claude LeBlanc really had caught the *fi-follet* in a bag. For if the *fi-follet* could turn into a giant, couldn't he just as easily turn into a mouse?

sashes red and blue

NEAR THE BEGINNING THE LE BLANCS LIVED AROUND Quebec, because that is where the first Le-Blanc settled with the gun and the cow and the wife given him by his King. But those early LeBlancs were a restless, daring tribe. Later some of them moved on to Montreal, then they went everywhere.

But the most restless and daring LeBlancs were those around Quebec and Montreal. The Quebec Le-Blancs wore long red sashes because that was the color for Quebec, and the Montreal LeBlancs wore long blue sashes because that was the color for Montreal.

To be sure, the LeBlancs were so restless that in later generations neither Quebec nor Montreal saw much of them. They were off in the woods working in the lumber camps. Or they were pushing up the river in great canoes looking for furs or fish or just looking for something new.

Sometimes blue-sashed LeBlancs met red-sashed LeBlancs, and then the rivalry was keen.

That's what happened up the Saguenay River when the lumber camp opened one winter. It was a bean for a pea because there were exactly as many Montreal LeBlancs as Quebec LeBlancs. Eight long blue sashes and eight long red sashes. Only the odds were one little bit against the red sashes because that unlucky Elphege LeBlanc was among them.

When there are blue sashes and red sashes so close together, there is bound to be one big fist-in-the-face after another.

All day the LeBlancs worked like sixteen beavers cutting down the trees. All night the LeBlancs quarreled and fought like sixteen wolves with one dead rabbit.

"A blue sash makes the best woodsman," said Henri LeBlanc, shaking the ashes from his pipe. "A red sash would do better running a store in Quebec."

"Bah!" said Elphege LeBlanc. "A blue sash makes a better dancing partner than a woodsman."

All sixteen LeBlancs began quarreling.

"We will let this decide itself," said old Paul LeBlanc. "A woodsman must be a good hunter. Sunday afternoon we will have one big moose hunt. That is, we will have two big moose hunts. The red-sashed Le Blancs will make one party and the blue-sashed LeBlancs will make the other. First party to get a moose is made of the best hunters. Do not feel too bad, red sashes. We will share our moose steaks with you."

So that Sunday afternoon the red sashes and the

blue sashes got whatever they used for guns and went out into the woods. The blue-sashed LeBlancs went in one direction and the red-sashed LeBlancs went in the other. All of the Quebec LeBlancs had some kind of a gun—all but Elphege. He carried the moose horn made of birch bark, because an unlucky man is better off with a horn instead of a gun. Besides, if Elphege was nothing else, he was a good moose caller.

The red sashes and their guns went this way and that way trying to find a moose to shoot.

"*Mma! Mma! Mma!*" bawled Elphege through his moose horn. Nothing answered but his echo.

For hours the brave hunters tramped through the woods looking for a moose.

At last Elphege and all his red-sashed companions

were happy to hear an answer to his horn which was not an echo.

"*Mma! Mma! Mma!*" came the answer to the moose horn.

It came from the other side of a rocky ridge. The men slowly crept up it with their guns ready.

Elphege blew his horn until his face was red so that the moose would not change its mind about meeting him.

"*Mma! Mma! Mma!*" came the answer. And over the rocky ridge came not a moose but the blue-sashed Henri LeBlanc with a moose horn to his own lips.

The red sashes and the blue sashes were so disappointed that for a sheep's wooden collar they would have had a shooting battle. But they tried to make the best of the thing, in the way of good woodsmen.

"Henri is a lucky man," said the blue sashes. "He might so easily have been shot for a moose by those stupid red sashes."

But the red sashes said, "Poor Elphege! We might have known he would be unlucky enough to call another moose caller instead of a moose."

For luck is judged by the company it keeps.

"We will try a different contest," said Paul Le-Blanc. "A woodsman must be a good tree cutter. You know that tall pine tree on the hill?"

All the LeBlancs nodded. Paul went on with his tongue.

"Tomorrow the red sashes will take the south side and the blue sashes will take the north. We will chop and chop until the tree falls. If it falls to the south, the red sashes have won because they have cut the farthest and the fastest. But of course the blue sashes will win because the tree will fall to the north."

Next morning the Montreal LeBlancs and the Quebec LeBlancs trudged on their snowshoes to the tall pine tree on the hill.

The Montreal LeBlancs took quick turns chopping on the north side, and the Quebec LeBlancs took quick turns chopping on the south side. Even the unlucky Elphege had no mishap with his ax.

The strength and speed of the LeBlancs was so equally divided that even when their axes met in the middle, the tree still stood. It was too evenly balanced to fall either way.

But a little gray squirrel, awakened from his winter sleep by the ax blows, went racing up to his hole to look out. His hole was on the south side. The weight of the squirrel set the tree to quivering and shaking. Slowly its crown began to lean over.

"We have won," cried a red sash. "Run for your lives!"

The red-sashed LeBlancs ran so fast that the tree missed everyone but that unlucky Elphege. The thong on his snowshoe came loose and tripped him up. A big branch knocked him to the ground and bruised his arms and broke his snowshoe in two.

"The squirrel cheated," cried Henri.

"The contest was unfair," shouted another blue sash. "Those Quebec LeBlancs must have put the squirrel inside the tree."

"Save your breath for the spring," said old Paul LeBlanc. "A woodsman must be good with a canoe paddle. When the river opens, we will have a canoe race to the St. Lawrence. First canoe to reach it carries the best LeBlancs."

It did not take too long for spring to come because the LeBlancs were kept so busy all winter. Only un-

lucky Elphege did not work well because his arms were still stiff from the blow they had received from the falling tree.

The LeBlancs launched two great birch canoes that spring, one full of red sashes and the other full of blue sashes.

"Away!" cried Elphege LeBlanc, the last one to step into his canoe.

But the canoe full of blue sashes was soon in the lead. Perhaps it was because of Elphege's stiff arms.

"This will never do," said Elphege. "Sooner than lose the race, we must go *chasse galerie*."

"What is that?" asked the LeBlanc in front of him.

"It is a trick I learned from Old Charlot, the devil," answered Elphege. "One time I had the bad luck to run into him in the woods. He was getting into his canoe so he did not see me. But I heard what he said to make it fly through the air."

The other LeBlancs were shocked by this, but they were a strong daring lot so they agreed to go *chasse galerie* to the St. Lawrence River.

Elphege solemnly recited the words he had heard Old Charlot use.

"Ma ne mi ne ma ne mo," he cried. "Up we go with Old Charlot."

Pou-i-i-iche went the great canoe as it shot up into the air.

One LeBlanc grabbed the thwarts and another Le-Blanc dropped his paddle. But Elphege, that unlucky one, was not quick enough to do anything because his arms were still stiff. He fell heels over head into the water. *Ploc!*

"Wait for me!" cried Elphege, splashing his stiff arms. "Wait for me!"

But already the great canoe was only a speck in the sky. At first the LeBlancs in the canoe did not know that Elphege had fallen out because his place in the stern was not empty. Then they saw that the boatman sitting there was not their relative. Elphege did not have a hooked tail and horns growing out of his fore-head. The man in the stern was no one but Old Charlot himself.

Old Charlot grinned at them wickedly.

"If it's a canoe ride you want, my sinners," he shouted, "I'll give you one that will never end."

The Quebec LeBlancs looked down and saw the

canoe of the blue sashes far below. And the Montreal LeBlancs looked up and thought they saw a wild goose flying in the wrong direction.

"If that honker doesn't come to earth before nightfall, he will bump into the moon," said one of the blue sashes. Then he paddled like mad so that the canoe of red sashes would not catch up with his own.

Old Charlot's canoe reached the St. Lawrence in no time. It flew on and on. Now the red sashes were paddling over Quebec. In no time they were over Three Rivers. In less time, they were over Montreal. They went as far as Detroit and then became lost in the clouds.

Sometimes the great canoe would fly low so that the people on earth could clearly see its shape.

If the people along the St. Lawrence saw the canoe, they would say, "The *chasse galerie!* It is those wicked men who went fishing on a Sunday."

People on the Detroit River sometimes saw the canoe on New Year's Eve. "The Canoe of the North," they would say. "In it are the souls of dead woodsmen returning for a last look at their homes and loved ones."

If a Frenchman fresh from France saw it, he would cry, "The *chasse galerie!* Regard the hunters riding their horses through the sky." Because those Frenchmen from France don't know a canoe from a horse. Wouldn't they be the fine ones to send into the Canadian woods?

But if the people along the Saguenay saw the canoe, they would cry, "The *chasse galerie!* Old Elphege LeBlanc has a crazy story about that ghost canoe. Poor, unlucky Elphege! He hasn't been the same since they fished him out of the river half drowned."

It has been many long years since anyone has seen the *chasse galerie*. My friends, Old Charlot's canoe must have caught itself in a cloud jam.

little Nichet's baby sister

THAT LITTLE NICHET, JEAN LE BLANC'S youngest child, was one to keep his parents as busy as all the other thirteen tied together.

One day the little fellow had a new question for his wise father.

"Papa," said Nichet, "where did the Boulangers get their new baby?"

"That is an easy question," answered Jean LeBlanc. "The good Indians brought her, my little nest egg."

"Did the good Indians bring me to you?" asked Nichet.

"Of course," answered his father. "The good Indians bring all the babies."

Little Nichet thought about this for a while.

"Papa," he asked again, "will the good Indians bring us another baby? I would like to have a little sister like Marie Boulanger."

"*Tatata!*" exclaimed Jean LeBlanc. "Already the good Indians have brought us a houseful. Thirteen brothers and sisters are quite enough for such a little fellow as you. And if we had a new baby, you would no longer be our little nest egg."

But Nichet did not think that thirteen brothers and sisters were enough, especially when they were all older and bigger than he.

One afternoon little Nichet wanted to ask his father more about this. But his father and his mother had driven to town in the two-wheeled cart with his eight sisters squeezed together in back.

It was a lonely day for Nichet because his five brothers were out in the field working. And Grandmère kept falling asleep over the rug she was hooking.

So Nichet bravely decided to go to the Indian village himself and ask the Indians if they didn't have an extra baby for the LeBlancs.

Nichet started out on his own two short legs. He walked down the river road. He walked up the Indian trail.

At last he came to the Indian village with its houses scattered over the ground like half-melons.

The Indian village was deserted. The Indians must have gone to town too. Then Nichet saw a few squaws working among the corn sprouts on the hillside. He started toward them.

But he never got as far as the cornfields. For there, propped against a tree trunk, was exactly what Nichet wanted. It was a little papoose laced to its cradle board.

Nichet was so excited that he could scarcely unlace the baby from the board. He lifted it carefully in his arms. The baby did not cry like the Boulanger's new Marie. Nichet looked at its brown skin and its black eyes and its straight black hair. He tried to decide whether it looked more like his papa or his mamma.

The little baby waved its tiny brown arms at him.

"You are my little sister," said Nichet. "I think you look most like me. I will take you home to your papa and mamma."

Nichet LeBlanc carried the papoose down the trail to the river road. It was a long walk and Nichet was so tired he did not think he would ever get the baby to its home. But his sturdy legs carried them both there at last.

Papa and Mamma and the girls had not returned from town yet. The boys were still in the field. Nichet took the baby to show her to Grandmère, but the old lady was asleep with her mouth open and her glasses on the end of her nose.

So little Nichet carried the baby into his parents' bedroom. He carefully laid it in the middle of the bright quilt. Then he ran down the lane to wait for his mamma and papa. He wanted to be the first one to tell them the news that they had a new baby.

At first his papa and mamma thought that little Nichet had a fever. Then they thought that he had fallen asleep like Grandmère and had had a bad dream. But when they saw the brown baby with the black hair and black eyes lying on the bed, they knew that Nichet had told the truth.

"Where did this baby come from?" cried Mamma LeBlanc.

"The Indians brought her," said little Nichet. "That is, I went and got her myself so they wouldn't give her to someone else."

Then there was a great *tohu-bohu* of chattering among the LeBlancs.

"We will have to take it right back," said Jean LeBlanc. "If the Indians think we have stolen their baby, they might burn down our house."

Little Nichet was brokenhearted. He begged and begged his parents to keep his little brown sister with the black hair and black eyes who looked so much like him.

But back to the Indians went the little sister. Little

Nichet held her in his arms all the way there in the two-wheeled cart.

There was another *tohu-bohu* of chattering going on at the Indian village.

"A bear has carried off one of the babies," a young brave explained to Jean LeBlanc.

"We have your baby here," said Jean. "It was carried off by a very little bear."

Nichet cried and cried at the loss of his Indian sister. He began feeling sorry for himself. He began thinking that if his papa and mamma had returned the baby to the Indians, they might do the same with him someday.

Little Nichet began feeling sorrier than ever for himself. He decided to return to the Indians of his own free will. How his parents would cry when they found he was gone! They would come galloping to the Indian village. They would take him home again —and his baby sister too.

He packed his nightshirt and his willow whistle and his lynx tail into a sack and set out for the Indian village once more. He walked all the way down the river road. He followed the trail to the houses that were like half-melons.

"I have come back to stay with my little sister," Nichet told one of the Indians.

Then the Indians were as worried as the LeBlancs had been.

"If we keep you here," said one of them, "your papa will think that we have stolen you. He will burn down our lodges."

Little Nichet refused to leave. "I want to stay here and be an Indian like my little sister," he said.

The Indians gathered together and talked their *micmac* talk, which Nichet could not understand. Then one of them turned to him.

"Can you shoot a bow and arrow?" he asked in Nichet's talk.

"No," said little Nichet.

"Can you skin a moose?"

"No," said little Nichet.

"Can you build a birch canoe?"

"No," said little Nichet.

"Then you cannot stay with us," said the brave. "An Indian must be able to do all those things."

So little Nichet sadly turned and started away. But

another Indian came running to him with something furry in his hands.

"A gift for you," said the Indian. "A trade for the baby you returned to us."

He dropped a tiny baby animal into Nichet's arms. It had the head of a beaver, the body of a bear, and the tail of a rabbit.

"What is it?" asked Nichet.

"Your wise father will have a name for it," said the Indian, then he began talking his *micmac* talk that Nichet could not understand.

Nichet carried the baby animal home happily. All the way his busy mind wondered if it was a fox or a beaver or a mink or what.

All the LeBlancs were happy to see that Nichet was home again. For truth, they didn't even know he had gone away until they saw the furry little animal in his arms.

"It is a little whistler," said his wise father, Jean LeBlanc. "Some people call them woodchucks and some people call them groundhogs. But the people back in France call them marmots."

"What is it good for?" asked Grandmère. "Will it

give milk or pull a cart or lay eggs?"

"It is good for a lonesome little boy who needs a companion smaller than himself," said Jean LeBlanc. He leaned over Nichet and smiled at the new baby. "Across the ocean in France," he said, "chimney sweeps from the mountains keep whistlers for pets. They teach them to do a little dance like a bear's."

"Can I be a chimney sweep when I am bigger?" asked little Nichet.

"You may be a chimney sweep tomorrow," said Jean LeBlanc generously. "I am going to take down the stovepipe for your mamma and you may help me clean the soot out of it."

So little Nichet thought that he had made a very good trade with the Indians. The boy picked out the name of Pierrette for his tiny pet, and his father helped him to teach that whistler to dance.

Whenever Nichet whistled a special tune, Pierrette would sit up on her hindquarters and wave her fore-paws from right to left as she did her dance of the bear. And from time to time she would make polite curtsies. You may be sure that Pierrette was as popular at the stay-awake parties as old Michel Meloche, the storyteller.

marionettes

ID SOMEBODY SAY THE NAME OF POLY-
carp LeBlanc? There was a man
with a voice as strong as his own two
arms. Tra lala ladera lala! That Polycarp
had a voice that could lift the roof. Good thing he
spent most of his time in the upper country with his
trap lines and his sled dogs.

It took a strong man to make those half-wild dogs
behave themselves. It was enough to frighten a bear
to see Polycarp clubbing his dogs to straighten them
out. But those dogs were so tough themselves that

they thought their master was giving them kind pats.

It was a sight for the snowshoe rabbits to see that team of five dogs pulling the sled along the trap lines with their tails riding high on their backs. And Polycarp running behind the sled as fast and as easily as a wild thing himself.

Up, up to the north he went in the winter, up to where the fur grew thickest and the snow lay deepest. Up, up toward the top of the world went Polycarp and his dogs to where the northern lights dance on their colored strings.

They say that when a man sees the dance of the marionettes, he must sing his loudest. Tra lala ladera lala! Because the louder he sings, the faster they will dance and they won't be able to bewitch him.

But one time Polycarp LeBlanc was having so much trouble with his dogs, he did not have time to look at the northern lights—let alone sing for them.

He had just finished making camp for the night. He had carefully counted the otter and fox skins on the sled. He had turned the dogs loose and cut fir branches for their beds. He had thrown them some half-frozen fish, then set up his own bed.

Scarcely had the trapper closed his tired, blurry eyes than the dance of the marionettes began in the sky.

The dogs woke up and began their wolflike howls. *"Hur-r-r-rle! Hur-r-r-rle!"* howled the dogs. It was enough to kill the top of the trapper's head.

So Polycarp started his own song.

"Tra lala ladera lala!" bawled Polycarp, and it was enough to kill the top of his dogs' heads.

The red and green marionettes danced madly. The dogs howled louder and louder. Polycarp sang louder and louder. He and his dogs made each other so wide awake that the trapper decided he might as well break camp and hit the trail. The sky was full of light so it was easy to pack the sled.

One by one, Polycarp called the dogs to harness. Only that leader dog, Loup, did not come at his call. The trapper began looking for him. There were dark hummocks of earth sticking up through the white

snow. Polycarp kicked one after another to see if it was his lead dog.

In the wink of an eye, one hummock jumped up and snarled at him. Polycarp brought his club down on the beast's savage head.

"You, Loup, you," he cried, "get yourself to the sled."

But the creature only snarled the more fiercely and leaped at the trapper's throat. Polycarp was outside of his patience by now.

He dropped the club and seized the animal's top jaw in his right hand and the bottom jaw in his left hand. He ground the long fangs together.

"If you want to bite Polycarp LeBlanc," said the trapper, "you will need sharper teeth."

The man let go of the strong jaws with his strong arms and picked up the club. The beast growled angrily and started to run away.

Polycarp caught its tail in his strong hand and swung it around and around. When it was dizzy, he grabbed it by the nape of the neck and dragged it to the sled.

The other dogs seemed angry with their leader too.

They all howled and jumped at him until they were as tangled as a bald eagle's nest. Polycarp clubbed each one in turn and then straightened them in their harness. He went to the back of the sled and took a firm hold of the handles.

"Mush, you bad dogs!" he cried. "Mush, you bad Loup."

The bad leader took off as if the northern lights were after his tail. And it was the same with the dogs behind him.

"Hoa!" cried Polycarp. "Not so fast." For he could scarcely hit the ground with his flying feet.

The marionettes were dancing on top of the world, but Polycarp's throat was so full of shouts for his dogs that there was no room for a song in it.

"You, Loup, you!" shouted the trapper. "Hoa!"

He glanced over his shoulder to see how much ground they had covered.

"Tra lala oh—tatata!" A dark-gray form was following across the white plain of snow. No wonder the dogs were in such a hurry.

"A wolf!" cried the trapper. "Wolves after us! Mush on, you dogs."

He cracked his whip over the dogs' tails that were riding high on their backs. They went even faster. First the sled was flying on one runner then it was flying on the other. The northern lights danced faster. The whole upper country seemed to be in flight from the wolfish figure chasing the sled.

"On, Loup!" shouted Polycarp, cracking his whip with fright.

And that leader went like a silver streak. But name of the *loup garou*, the gray beast was getting closer and closer.

Polycarp saw that he would have to make a last stand.

His strong arms and his strong voice stopped the dogs. He grabbed his gun from the sled. He pointed it at the gray beast, which was almost on him.

"*Pan*," went the gun, but the marionettes were dancing so madly that his eyes were dancing too. He missed the beast once and he missed it twice. Before he could fire a third shot, its great body leaped at him.

Polycarp was thrown to the ground. The beast jumped on him. It buried its claws in his chest. Then it began licking his cold face with its warm tongue. It looked softly at him with its big brown eyes.

"Loup," cried the trapper. "It's Loup."

He sat up and stared at the leader so patiently waiting for his next command.

"A wild wolf!" cried Polycarp. "I have hitched a wild wolf with my dog team."

Polycarp jumped up and seized his gun again.

"Another skin to add to my catch," he cried triumphantly.

He pointed the gun at the gray wolf. He looked down the long barrel into the pale-gray eyes. My faith, why hadn't he noticed those gray eyes before? He looked at the friendly grin spreading across the long red tongue. Then Polycarp dropped his gun to his side.

He unhitched the wolf and put Loup back in his rightful place. He patted the wolf with his hand instead of his club.

"Begone!" said Polycarp to the wolf firmly. "And take your skin with you or I'll be putting it in my sled with the otters and foxes."

Then he remembered the northern lights.

"Tra lala ladera lala!" sang Polycarp in his strongest voice.

The marionettes danced like mad. They danced to the right and they danced to the left, all in such perfect time to the trapper's song. They danced faster and faster until they disappeared over the top of the world. And so did the wolf that Polycarp's strong arms had trained to harness in such a short time.

"Blue moose!" cried Polycarp, rubbing his sleepy, blurry eyes. "I do not believe tonight happened."

When he returned to civilization, no one else believed that such a night had happened either.

"Polycarp LeBlanc says he hitched a wild wolf to his sled in place of his lead dog, Loup," they said. "His imagination is as strong as his voice and his arms."

That dance of the marionettes has bewitched more than one man in the upper country.

the hard master

THEY STILL REMEMBER ON THE ÎLE D'ORLÉANS how Pitou LeBlanc learned a lesson from a horse. Pitou was a hard master to his farm animals. And his bad temper made things worse for his ox, Napoleon, and his horse, Josephine.

"Beasts were made to work for men," said Pitou. "I am no fool like my grandfather who pulled the plow beside his ox."

It had taken some time for the horse and the ox to learn to work together as teammates. An ox pulls with a long, steady stride. A horse pulls in jerks.

One day when Pitou LeBlanc was all set to drive a load of hay to the Besette farm, Josephine went lame from working so long and hard beside an ox.

Pitou hurried to the farm of his neighbor, old Joseph Rivard.

"May I borrow your Olinde to help pull a load of hay over to my father-in-law's farm?" he asked. "My Josephine has a sickness of the hoofs and spirit."

Joseph Rivard did not want to lend his horse to Pitou LeBlanc. He did not think that he was a fair master to his beasts. But the farmer was his neighbor, and it does not make for good feeling to refuse a neighbor help.

"I will make one rule if you use my Olinde," he finally stated. "You must not touch her with the whip. I have never struck Olinde myself because she is like a daughter to me in my old age."

"Horses and daughters are easily spoiled," said Pitou. "But I solemnly promise that I will not whip Olinde."

The plan seemed agreeable to the horse at the very beginning. She went willingly enough down the road with her new master. *Cloump, cloump*, went her bearded hoofs.

Pitou led her to his shed, where Napoleon was already harnessed to the big hay wagon.

Olinde stood quietly while Pitou buckled Josephine's collar around her neck. She stood quietly while he pulled her thick tail through the crupper. But when Pitou led her into place beside the wooden tongue of the wagon, Olinde looked at Napoleon as if she had never seen such a beast before.

"*Heni-i-i-ise!*" she protested.

Pitou reached for the chain that hooked to the whiffletree of the wagon. Olinde started to dance sideways. The farmer was in a sweat and out of half of his patience by the time he was able to fasten the chain. He screwed his lips together so that his temper would not jump out.

He wiped the sweat from his forehead, climbed up on the seat of the wagon, and twisted the reins around his hands.

"*Gioc!*" he shouted. "Giddap!"

Napoleon started his long, steady steps. Olinde started her jerky ones. Out of step and out of spirit, the team got as far as the main road.

Then Olinde pressed her ears against her head. She braced her hoofs against the ground so that she was almost sitting on the whiffletree.

Napoleon stopped pulling and gave her a reproachful look through his long, pale eyelashes. Olinde rolled her own eyes around until nothing showed but the whites.

Pitou LeBlanc gave her a gentle push with the ox goad.

"*Gioc*, Olinde!" he shouted.

Olinde snorted. Her right hind leg jumped over the chain.

Pitou LeBlanc put the goad in its socket because he could not trust himself. He jumped down from the wagon and lifted Olinde's right hind leg back across the chain. He grabbed Olinde's reins on both sides of the bit in her mouth.

"*Gioc!*" he thundered, as he pulled on the bit.

Olinde tossed her mouth from side to side and pulled back until her ears slipped out of the bridle. She sat down heavily on the whiffletree.

The farmer let go of his patience.

"Name of a donkey!" he cried. "I will show you something, Joseph Rivard's horse. I will show you how a beast should work for his master."

He angrily unfastened the chain. He pulled Olinde away from the wagon. He tore Josephine's harness off her.

Pitou pulled the big collar over his own head. He fastened the chain to the whiffletree. And he was in such a rage that he did not mind that the collar did not fit him properly nor that the crupper dragged behind him in the dust.

He took Napoleon by one long curved horn.

"*Gioc*, Napoleon," he cried.

Olinde watched the lesson on how a horse should behave. She stretched her neck, turned her ears all the way forward, and stared from under her heavy bangs. She watched the patient Napoleon pulling the heavy hay wagon with the impatient Pitou LeBlanc for a teammate.

"Now go home, you good-for-what horse," cried Pitou. "Tell your master that if he had any sense he would lay the whip to you now and then."

The wagon creaked and groaned. Napoleon plodded on steadily. Pitou LeBlanc was straining so hard at Josephine's collar that his eyes were popping.

Olinde did not go home. She saw that the wagon was piled high with sweet, fresh hay. She started to follow it. She tore off a wisp of the sweet, fresh hay.

Down the road went the creaking wagon with Napoleon and his master pulling it. Behind followed Olinde, greedily eating the hay.

People ran to their doors to gape. Dogs ran to their gates to bark. Old Grandpère LaFrance laughed so hard that Grandmère was afraid he would have a stroke.

The strange turnout paraded through the village.

"Regard the team pulling the hay wagon," cried the storekeeper, who was sitting on the porch of his store. "Which is the man and which is the ox?"

This insult made Pitou LeBlanc so angry that he had the strength of two Napoleons. The big ox could scarcely keep up with him.

At last the ill-mated team drove into the Besette farmyard. All the Besettes came out to see the sight. It was the only time that Madame Besette ever let fritters burn on her stove.

"Why is not Olinde sitting up in the driver's seat?" asked Jean Besette.

"What a question!" panted Pitou. "That lazy good-for-what horse is back in her barn by now."

Olinde knew this was not true.

"*Henisse*," she whinnied.

It was not a very loud whinny because she was so full of hay. She had nibbled a cave into the wagon.

Pitou freed himself from his harness. His tired,

wobbly legs carried him behind the wagon.

Anger spun around in his head like a red wheel. It burst into a thousand pieces.

He snatched the goad out of its socket. He broke the promise which he had tried so hard to keep. He brought the goad down on Olinde's plump back with one big *clac*.

The horse was so frightened and surprised that she took to her bearded hoofs. She galloped down the road as if the goblin *lutin* were riding her.

But Olinde could not keep up her mad pace. She was too gorged with hay. She felt a little pain in her stomach. She stopped galloping. The pain in her stomach grew bigger. She stopped trotting. The pain in her stomach felt as big as she.

Olinde gave a groan. She sat down at the side of the road. She gave another groan and rolled into the ditch.

That is where Pitou LeBlanc found her. He was driving back from the Besette barn. He sat on the driver's seat where he belonged. Now that the wagon was empty, Napoleon could pull it by himself.

Pitou LeBlanc was full of shame. He ran all the

way to Joseph Rivard's farm because he could get there faster on foot than behind Napoleon. In the village he left a message for the horse doctor.

"I tell you, Joseph," he almost wept, "it was not my fault. If Olinde had been a well-raised and reasonable horse, it never would have happened."

The horse doctor and half the village were with Olinde when they reached her.

"It is a bad case of colic," the horse doctor told Joseph Rivard. "You are feeding her too much rich provender. Just because you are a prosperous farmer, you don't have to feed your horse to death."

He did not listen to old Joseph's explanation. He forced Olinde's mouth open and poured a whole bottle of bitter, brown medicine down her throat. Olinde groaned more loudly than ever.

"Now we must get her up on her feet and keep her there," said the horse doctor.

Pitou LeBlanc groaned himself as he helped pull Olinde to her feet.

"Take her home and keep walking her," said the horse doctor to old Joseph Rivard. "When a sick horse lies down too long, she dies of despair. And remember what I said. Stop stuffing your horse with grain just because you had a good harvest this year."

"Perhaps you could give me some medicine, too," said Pitou LeBlanc to the horse doctor. "I ache all over and my neck is stiff."

The horse doctor snapped his bag shut.

"Ha!" he snorted. "All you need is a diet of raw oats and some exercise."

Pitou LeBlanc went with Joseph and Olinde back to the Rivard farm while his father-in-law took charge of Napoleon and the empty hay wagon.

Joseph Rivard was so old and so upset by it all that he was no help. It became Pitou's job to keep Olinde on her feet. He pulled and pulled at her bridle. He pushed and pushed at her tail. All the rest of the afternoon he sweated and stayed red in the face.

When he thought that he would surely drop down and die himself, Olinde stopped groaning. A bright light came into her dulled eyes. She gave two loud hiccoughs.

Then she kicked up her heels, switched her tail, and jerked away from Pitou.

"*Heni-i-isse!*" she whinnied joyfully.

She went trotting off toward the barn.

"Bless that horse doctor!" exclaimed Joseph Rivard. "Without his good medicine, Olinde never would have pulled through."

"Bless me, too," gasped Pitou LeBlanc, "because it is I who have done all of Olinde's pulling for her. Believe me, I will think a long time before I give Napoleon and Josephine such heavy loads to pull again."

"That is as it should be," said Joseph Rivard. "A man must feel the weight of a beast's load before he can be a good master."

how little Nichet
became Jean-Baptiste

O YOU CHILDREN WANT TO HEAR MORE about little Nichet.

When autumn came and the days grew colder, Nichet's pet whistler Pierrette became fat and lazy. It was hard to get her to do her clever dance of the bear. Then one day, she slowly waddled to the mop in the corner of the kitchen. She crawled into the ragged folds and went to sleep. She slept and she slept and she slept.

She wouldn't awaken for Nichet or Jean LeBlanc or even for Mamma when she wanted to use the mop

65

on the kitchen floor. Madame LeBlanc had to use an old rag when she washed the floor.

Little Nichet wept his eyes red. He thought that his pet was dead. But his wise father, Jean LeBlanc, knew what was wrong with Pierrette.

"Whistlers sleep all winter long, my little nest egg," said Jean. "The days are growing shorter and colder so Pierrette knows it is time to go to sleep. She will wake up again next spring and dance for us all."

"Why don't we sleep all winter too?" little Nichet asked his father. "Why?"

"Yes, why, why?" asked all the fourteen LeBlancs, who were so good at making questions.

"Because if we slept through the winter," said Jean LeBlanc, "we would miss Christmas and the first Day of the Year."

Then all the little LeBlancs were glad it was Pierrette sleeping away the months in the mop and not themselves. Christmas and the Day of the Year were the two biggest days on the calendar. Every day they marked off the date on the old calendar in the kitchen so they would bring the two big days faster.

Winter came early to Canada that year. There were many snowstorms and freeze-ups. Winter brought sledding and ice-skating to the LeBlanc house on the farm. It brought something else to the house.

One cold day little Marie-Elaine came home from school with a runny nose and a fever. Next day red spots broke out on her face and her chest. The next day after that, Dr. Lemaire came in his sleigh.

"It is the measles," said Dr. Lemaire. Then he looked at the thirteen other children. "Don't look so sad in the face," he said. "You will not be overlooked. You will surely get the measles too."

Then something worse than the measles happened. Mamma LeBlanc packed a basket with some of her clothes and Jean LeBlanc hitched the old horse to the cradle sleigh.

"Are you leaving us?" cried all the little LeBlancs.

"Mamma must go and stay with her sister in town," said Jean. "She has never had the measles like Grand-mère and me. We wouldn't want our plump, pretty mamma to get the measles, would we?"

Then the LeBlanc children began to weep like calves. They didn't want Mamma to get the measles and they didn't want her to leave them. Worst of all, Christmas was coming on the calendar.

But Jean LeBlanc hurried their mother away in the sleigh. The children howled and howled all the louder.

"Who will take care of us?" cried little Nichet.

Their Grandmère was quite put out of herself. "Do you think that after raising eighteen of my own I am not able to take care of fourteen more?" she asked.

Dr. Lemaire was right. One after another of the LeBlancs got the measles from Marie-Elaine. Little Nichet looked at the red spots on his own chest and arms.

"Where do the measles come from?" he asked his Grandmère.

"From all the questions inside children," said Grandmère, who was so busy trying to do everything at once. "They come out in big red spots."

Little Nichet wished he hadn't been so full of questions, especially near Christmas time. Now there would be no going to church in the cradle sleigh in the middle of the night with a big stay-awake party after their return.

There was something else that bothered little Nichet's head, but he tried not to think about it. He didn't want to break out in any more red spots.

Jean LeBlanc helped his children get ready for Christmas as if the measles had never happened.

He made a little stable out of an old store box and thatched its roof with hay. Then the children helped him dig down into the old wooden chest in the attic for the holy figures their grandfather had carved. Long, long ago he had carved them, when there had been eighteen little LeBlancs instead of fourteen.

There were brightly painted figures of the Christ child and Mary and Joseph. There were brightly painted figures of shepherds and sheep and dogs. There were brightly painted figures of the Three Wise Men on their camels, but they had to stay in the chest until it was time for them to arrive at the stable of Bethlehem.

What little Nichet liked best of all, next to the Christ child, was a *petit* little mouse, no bigger than a question mark, which Grandpère must have carved from a splinter.

"Your Grandpère said there were always mice in

his barn," explained Jean LeBlanc to his children, "so there must have been at least one mouse in the stable of Bethlehem."

Little Nichet, because he was the youngest, got to lay the Christ child in the manger bed. And as an extra treat he was also allowed to put the *petit* little mouse where he wished. He put it up on the edge of the manger because there were so many times when, lying in his bed with measles, he had wished for Pierrette or even a mouse to entertain him.

At last he couldn't keep his question inside him any more.

"Papa," he asked, "will the Christ child come into

our house New Year's Eve when we are asleep and leave presents in our shoes like He always does?"

"You wouldn't want the little Christ child to get your measles, would you?" asked Jean LeBlanc. "Wouldn't that be a fine present for Him?"

"You mean we won't get any presents this year?" cried Marie-Elaine, who was already over her measles.

"I'm sure that the Christ child will leave your presents with your mamma," said Grandmère.

So you can know how dull it was for those little LeBlancs. On Christmas Eve, they didn't even stay awake to watch the sleighs go racing past their house full of happy people on their way to the church in the village. They didn't see the lanterns carried by those on foot. They didn't hear the great church bells ringing. They didn't even hear the excited voices at their own door. The little LeBlancs had gone to bed very early to quickly put an end to such an unhappy day.

In other years, the little LeBlancs had always eagerly awaited the Day of the Year. It was the biggest holiday in French Canada. It began with the visit of the Guignolée on New Year's Eve. They were men wearing masks and carrying stout sticks. They went from house to house gathering gifts of money and food and clothing for the poor of the parish. There was always a fiddle among them and perhaps a tambourine or two. They came inside the houses and sang songs and ate cakes with the families. Oh, it was fun!

Again the Guignolée came to the LeBlanc house in their big sledge. They stood outside in the snow and sang an old song. The song warned that if the people in the house gave them nothing, the Guignolée would carry off the oldest daughter.

Then they knocked on the door with their stout sticks.

Jean LeBlanc, followed by all his children who were out of bed, went to the door with lamp in hand. He flung the door open while the children stared big eyes at the masked men.

"I am sorry," said Jean LeBlanc, "but I cannot invite you into this house. We have nothing to give but the measles. If you want to carry off my oldest daughter, you will have to take her from her bed."

So the Guignolée quickly climbed back in their

sledge without taking Marie-Louise. They did not want the measles for the poor or themselves.

The Day of the Year, Mamma was still away. But Papa came to the children's room early and saw that they were all up and neatly dressed, even Marie-Louise.

"The blessing," he reminded them. "We must receive Grandmère's blessing for the new year."

Jean LeBlanc formed them into a line with Pierre-Paul at the head and little Nichet making the tail. He marched them to Grandmère's room, which suddenly seemed as holy as the sanctuary at church.

Grandmère had just finished putting her round black cap on her gray hair. Jean LeBlanc asked her blessing for all of them. They went down on their knees to receive it.

Grandmère raised the thin, wrinkled hands that had taken care of so many little LeBlancs. She gave the kneeling family her blessing.

"And may God make you happy and prosperous in the new year," she ended. "And if it is not possible for Him to make you prosperous on such a small, poor farm, may He make you happy and healthy."

After she had given her blessing, Grandmère put her old arm around little Nichet. "I do not believe measles are caused by questions, Jean-Baptiste," she said. "I think they are something Old Charlot lets loose from his bag."

Little Nichet was astonished. Not because the measles came out of a bag, but because his Grand-mère had called him Jean-Baptiste. He hadn't been called that big name since the priest himself had given it to him at his baptism.

The children pressed the buttons of their noses against the window as they watched the sleighs go by filled with gay, laughing people making calls on their

friends. Of course, none of the sleighs stopped in front of their house.

Grandmère tried to make it gay for them. She had cooked *croquignoles*, those Christmas cakes so like the doughnuts of these United States. She had even made a cake of her own idea that was covered with raisins stuck on toothpicks. It looked like the forest where Papa went to cut wood in the winter when his children didn't have the measles.

But all the cakes in Canada couldn't fill the empty place left by Mamma.

So Christmas and the Day of the Year went past the LeBlanc children as if they had been asleep in the mop with little Nichet's whistler.

But unhappy things have to come to an end sometime. Sorrow and loneliness and the measles can't last forever. They run their course and then go on to somebody else.

One day when the sun was shining on the snow and the last measle had gone away, Jean LeBlanc hitched the old horse to the sleigh and set out to get Mamma. And that seemed the longest day of the year, with the little LeBlancs pressing the buttons of their noses against the window and waiting so impatiently for Mamma.

"Do you think she will remember the presents from the Christ child?" asked Nichet of his Grandmère, who was busily running from stove to table.

"Answer me a question, Jean-Baptiste," said Grandmère. "If the Christ child gave you a present to give your mamma, would you forget it?"

Nichet shook his head. Then it happened. All the little LeBlancs began dancing around like Pierrette on her hind legs.

"Mamma!" they shouted. "Mamma is coming!"

The cradle sleigh was coming up the lane. And there was Mamma sitting beside Papa. And in her arms were the presents from the Christ child all wrapped carefully in a blanket.

The children danced and danced while Papa helped Mamma out of the sleigh. They danced and flung the door open and cried to their mother:

"Blessed Christmas, Mamma!"

"A happy and holy year, Mamma!"

"The measles are all gone, Mamma!"

Mamma carried the presents from the Christ child

carefully. When the door had been closed so there would be no draft, she lifted an edge of the blanket. There was a tiny new baby. A little, red, wrinkled baby with eyes closed like Pierrette's. A fifteenth little LeBlanc to grow up and ask questions.

"Your new brother," said Mamma proudly.

"Did the good Indians bring him?" asked little Nichet. Only he couldn't be the little nest egg any longer now. That was why Grandmère had been calling him Jean-Baptiste.

"Poush!" said Mamma. "Would the good Indians bring a baby on Christmas Eve? Of course not. This little one is your special present from the Little Jesus because you were such good children the past year."

They all pressed close to the new baby and touched his fingers that were no bigger than the mouse in the Christmas stable.

Then Mamma knelt on the floor with the new baby in her arms and received the blessing from Grandmère, because no one is ever too late to be blessed by the oldest member of the family.

It was Jean-Baptiste who got to hold the baby first. He sat very straight in the big rocking chair and slowly rocked the new little Nichet back and forth.

"Look at them!" said Grandmère. "They are like two heads in one bonnet."

The big brother was proud that he was now Jean-Baptiste. He felt full of the health and happiness that Grandmère's blessing had asked for him.

Never, never, thought Jean-Baptiste, had the Le-Blancs had such a wonderful Christmas and first Day of the Year.

the *lutin* in the barn

I T IS A LONG TIME SINCE THE "LUTIN" HAS BEEN seen in Canada. That is not because the horses have turned into automobiles. French Canada is still a place for horses on farms and on the roads. It must be Tonton LeBlanc who drove the *lutin* away forever.

Tonton had the fastest horse in the Beauce. His Rosa-mai won all the races in that part of the country. Once a week there would be a big race with every farmer for miles around riding his best horse.

The prize was always a bag of potatoes or a sack of flour.

It was too bad that Tonton had no family. He could have fed a wife and twenty children with all the potatoes and flour that his fast horse Rosa-mai won in the races.

Tonton didn't think that he needed a wife or children as long as he had Rosa-mai. He moved to a little room over the stable so he could be close to his horse and watch her at all times. He had a great fear that some night a thief would break into his barn and steal Rosa-mai.

One morning Tonton LeBlanc went down to feed his horse her oats.

To his great surprise, Rosa-mai was wearily leaning her head against the manger as if her legs couldn't hold her up. Her black coat was covered with white sweat. Her long mane was tangled in untidy loops.

Tonton was horrified. He wiped her off carefully with his own towel. He combed her mane carefully with his own comb.

"Some rascal has been riding you," he said to Rosa-mai. "Who was he?"

Of course he received no answer, and he didn't really expect one.

Tonton LeBlanc lifted her hoofs, one after another. Aha! He was right. A shoe was gone from her left hind foot.

Tonton let her rest and eat her oats. Then he put the bridle on her head and the saddle on her back. He rode to the blacksmith's shop in the village.

He found the blacksmith busy at his forge. He was surrounded by the usual men who had nothing to do but stand around in the blacksmith shop and chew pigtail tobacco.

Tonton told the blacksmith about the sad way in which he had found his horse that morning.

The men with nothing to do crowded around him. They looked at Rosa-mai's hoof with the shoe missing. They looked at her damp black coat. They looked at her thick mane and, my faith, the untidy loops were still there, although Tonton had combed them out so carefully.

"The *lutin* is riding her," said one of the men.

"The loops will not comb out of her mane until it rains again," said another.

"*Tatata!*" exclaimed Tonton. "A likely cock-and-donkey story! Some young rascal in the countryside is riding her. I will catch him tonight."

That night Tonton LeBlanc laid a trap for the rascal who was riding his horse. He got a ball of string. He tied one end of it to the handle of the barn door. He unwound the ball through the stable, up the ladder, under his door, over the floor to his bed. When he went to bed, he put his gun on the floor beside him. Then he tied the other end of the string to his big toe.

"When the rascal pulls the stable door open," he told his gun, "it will jerk my toe. Then it will be your turn to do something."

Tonton LeBlanc closed his eyes and fell fast asleep. He slept as soundly as an old shoe. When he opened his eyes again, it was morning. His toe was still there and his gun was still there. He knew that Rosa-mai was still there, too, because he could hear her snuffling below him.

He untied the string from his toe, dressed himself, and climbed down the ladder.

There was Rosa-mai with her head leaning against the manger again. Her black coat was covered with white sweat and there were more loops in her mane. The string across the stable had been cut in two. How had the rascal managed to do that?

Tonton was mad like two wolves.

He vowed that he would not sleep a wink the next night. And he kept that vow. *Parbleu*, how he kept that vow!

He blew out his lantern so the rascal riding Rosa-mai would think he was asleep. He laid flat on the floor with his ear to a crack.

As his big clock struck twelve, there was a great *berdi-berda* in the stable below. He heard Rosa-mai whinny shrilly and kick at the door. Then, *hélas!* He couldn't find a match to light the lantern right away.

His angry, trembling hand was just making a light when he heard Rosa-mai back out of the stable.

Tonton LeBlanc only had time to run to the window with the lantern. He opened it and leaned out. Rosa-mai came galloping below him. Tonton turned the lantern on her. A-tou-tou-tou! On her back was a monster covered with long hair. He had the face of an ape and the horns of a cow.

It was the *lutin*.

He rode without a saddle. His great claws were twisted in Rosa-mai's mane to keep him from falling off.

As the horse raced below Tonton's window, the *lutin* let go with one paw and waved to the man at the window.

"Since you are awake," he called, "I'll be back in an hour for a game of cards."

Tonton LeBlanc was terrified. He wished he had never seen his rascal. He bolted the door. Against it he pushed all the bags of potatoes and sacks of flour he had won in the races.

It seemed that he waited hours and hours in the fort of flour and potatoes.

Suddenly he heard Rosa-mai's flying hoofs. He heard the barn door groan open. He heard the ladder creak and creak.

There was a *toc, toc* on the door.

"Go away," cried Tonton.

"If I go away, I'll take your horse with me," threatened the *lutin*. "I will never bring her back."

Tonton LeBlanc was not a very brave man, but he loved his beautiful black horse dearly. My faith, hadn't he given up a big, warm house to live in a loft over her stable? He did not want the *lutin* to ride her away forever.

He took his heart in his two hands, as we say of brave people. He moved the bags of potatoes and the sacks of flour from the door.

He opened it and in walked the ugly *lutin* as if he were an invited guest. He looked all around Tonton's little room.

"Humph!" he snorted. "I've seen better stables than this." He walked over to the table and sat down on the stool. "Where are the cards?"

Tonton took a worn pack of cards from his drawer. He pulled up a bag of potatoes and sat down on it.

"Shall we play 'seven up'?" he asked.

The *lutin* shook his horns. "A game for cowherds," he snapped. "We will play 'slap Jacques.' I'll deal because I don't trust you."

The *lutin* riffled the cards between his long claws.

He dealt one card to himself, one to Tonton, one to himself, one to Tonton. When he had finished dealing, he picked up his hand with his long claws. He threw a card on the table. Tonton dropped another on top of it.

The *lutin* leaned over the table and peeped into Tonton's hand. "Why don't you play your Jacques?" he asked.

"You are cheating," said Tonton. But he took the card back and laid the jack of spades on the table. "Slap Jacques," he said, tapping the cards lightly.

The *lutin* brought his huge claws down on Tonton's knuckles.

"SLAP JACQUES," he bawled. "*My* trick."

"You have the manners of the stable, monsieur," said Tonton, rubbing his hand.

"And you have poor manners for a host," retorted the *lutin*. "Don't you offer food to your company?"

Tonton laid his hand down and rose from the sack of potatoes.

"I have some cold potato pie left from supper," he said. "I eat it three times a day to try to get rid of all the flour and potatoes I win in races."

Tonton went into the nook which served as his kitchen. He began cutting the cold, soggy potato pie. As he did so, he raised his eyes to the tin mirror hanging over the shelf. He looked at his scared, tired face.

Then an idea jumped from the mirror into Tonton's head. His face didn't look so tired and scared any more.

He cut two pieces of pie and then he cut a third piece of pie. He put each piece on a cracked plate. He carried them out to the table on which laid the cards.

The *lutin* looked at the three pieces of pie. "Why do you bring me two pieces?" he asked. "From the messy look of it, I will be doing good to force one down my gullet."

Tonton hummed a little tune. "I cut three pieces of pie because I am expecting a friend to join us shortly," he replied.

The *lutin* was interested. "Does he have a horse?" he asked.

"I don't know," said Tonton, "but he is one of the best horsemen in Canada."

The *lutin* was more interested than ever. "Do I know him?" he asked.

"You should," answered Tonton. "He is a well-known fellow. Only a few days ago all the men in the blacksmith shop were talking about him."

"What is his name?" asked the *lutin*.

"I only know his nickname," said Tonton. "I don't believe he has a Christian name." He seemed to get a sudden idea. "Come to think of it, I have a picture of him hanging in my kitchen," he said. "I will show it to you."

Tonton LeBlanc went to the nook and took the mirror down from the wall. He carried it to the *lutin*. He put it in his long claws.

"Does the face look familiar?" asked Tonton.

The *lutin* looked into the mirror. He saw the ape-like face and the long horns growing out of the head. He threw the mirror on the table in fright. He jumped up from the stool.

"*Tondu!*" he cried. "Your friend is an ugly monster. I am not staying around here to meet *him*."

And the *lutin* was so frightened by the hideous face he had seen that he didn't even take time to go out the door and down the ladder. He jumped right through the window, glass and all.

Tonton LeBlanc carried the mirror down to the stable and hung it over his horse's manger—just in case the *lutin* should come back.

But the *lutin* never came back to Tonton's stable, and the next time it rained all the loops combed out of Rosa-mai's mane. The wonder of it was that the *lutin* never came back to the Beauce any more. Perhaps that was the last time he was ever seen in Canada. He wasn't taking any chances of meeting that ugly monster face to face.

the sheep with
the wooden collar

LITTLE JEAN-BAPTISTE LE BLANC BEGAN FEEL-ing like one big man when he had a brother smaller than himself. The new Nichet was not a playmate for him yet, but Jean-Baptiste did not mind that.

He carried his little brother about in his arms. He talked to him and sang a song to him about a gray hen who laid her *coco* in the church just for Nichet.

When all the LeBlancs went to a stay-awake party given by the neighbors, Jean-Baptiste was made the special watcher of the new little nest egg. Now that he was such a big boy, he was able to stay awake later at the parties. He was able to sing songs with the others and listen to the exciting stories told by the old heads. Stories about fearsome *loups garous* and *lutins* and *fi-follets*.

Jean-Baptiste began wishing he could tell such stories. He often thought about this as he rocked his little brother or played with his pet whistler, who woke up in the spring and still remembered how to dance.

He thought about the exciting stories as he did his chores around the farmhouse. He was thinking about them the day his father sent him and the dog Toutou to the river pasture to drive home the sheep.

Jean-Baptiste leaned on the woven fence that leaned on the ground.

He watched the sheep nibbling the fresh grass and bleating about nothing at all. He watched the marbly-eyed gray sheep who wore a wooden collar around her neck.

"That sheep has a mind of her own," his father had said. "It is not bad for a cow or a chicken or a horse to have a mind of its own. But when a sheep has a mind of her own, she begins jumping over fences."

So the sheep with her own mind had to wear a wooden collar so she couldn't jump over the woven fence.

She had her own mind with her this late afternoon. "*Moute, moute!*" Jean-Baptiste called to the sheep.

All the other sheep were ready to follow tails home, but the one with the wooden collar had her own idea. She ran back and forth across the pasture, lifting her hoofs and lifting her tail.

Toutou was right behind her, nipping at her hoofs as they went up and down. First she ran away to the north. Then she turned east. Finally she turned south and followed the other sheep to the road.

Jean-Baptiste thought about this as he and Toutou walked in the dust of the sheep.

"Bê! Bê!" bleated the other sheep in a chorus, as if they were singing a round.

But the sheep with the mind of her own didn't sing one "bê." She tossed her wooden collar. She lifted her hoofs and she lifted her tail. She ran along by herself.

Jean-Baptiste decided to make his story about her.

As his worn moccasins scuffed in the dusty sheep tracks, his mind made up the story. He could hardly wait to get home to tell it to his father.

He didn't have to wait that long. Luc Boulanger came driving his two-wheeled cart toward them. When he met the sheep, he saw that he couldn't go any farther until they were past him. So he stopped his horse.

The sheep on the right wanted to pass him on the left. The sheep on the left wanted to pass him on the right. They bumped into each other and followed tails around Luc Boulanger's cart. They made two streams of wool, as if the cart were a canoe in the middle.

"Bê! Bê!" bleated the sheep following tails.

But the sheep with the wooden collar didn't say a single "bê." She just lifted her hoofs and lifted her tail until she came to Luc Boulanger's horse. Then she dropped her hoofs and she dropped her tail. She would not go any farther. Luc Boulanger snapped at her with his whip, but that only frightened his horse.

"That is a stubborn sheep you have there," said Luc to Jean-Baptiste.

Jean-Baptiste put his hands in his pockets and looked up at Luc.

"She is a very strange sheep also," said the boy. "I did not think I would get her this close to home. She wouldn't leave the pasture with the other sheep. She ran north and grew as big as a yearling calf. She turned east and grew as big as a horse. She turned south and grew as big as a house. So, believe me, the other sheep and I started to run down this road as fast as our feet would take us. And Toutou ran too. He was afraid of that sheep as big as a house."

Luc Boulanger's eyes were almost as big as his ears at this tale. He backed his horse way over to the side of the road. He squeezed himself into the farthest end of the seat as the sheep with the wooden collar went by, lifting her hoofs and lifting her tail.

Jean-Baptiste and Toutou drove the sheep up the LeBlanc lane to the barn. The boy opened the door and the dog drove the sheep through it.

Then the little boy kicked up his moccasins like a frolicky lamb himself. He ran to find his father. He found him mending a broken hoe near the back door.

Jean-Baptiste put his hands in his pockets and looked up into his father's face.

"Papa," he said, "something very strange happened today."

"Did that sheep jump the fence even with the wooden collar on her neck?" asked Jean LeBlanc.

"No, Papa, it was stranger than that," said the boy. "When I went with Toutou to get the sheep, she tried to run away from us. She ran north and grew big as a yearling calf. She turned east and grew big as a horse. She turned south and grew big as a house. It really stretched my eyes, Papa."

"My faith," cried Jean LeBlanc. "The sheep is bewitched. I always thought there was something strange about a sheep having a mind of her own. Do not go near her alone."

All the other LeBlancs were told about the sheep.

"She ran north and got big as a yearling calf," repeated Jean-Baptiste, with his hands in his pockets. "She turned east and grew big as a horse. She turned south and grew big as a house."

The little LeBlancs began to howl.

"She is a *loup garou*," cried Marie-Elaine. "We are living on a farm with a *loup garou*."

"The *lutin* must be riding her," cried Pierre-Paul.

Mamma was sitting in the rocking chair feeding the new Nichet some gruel. She held the baby closer so that the sheep could not get him.

"Poush!" said Grandmère. "A sheep is a sheep. How could a stupid sheep grow big as a horse or a house? Come here, Jean-Baptiste. Let me feel your forehead. Perhaps you have a fever."

But no one listened to Grandmère because a fever is a dull thing while a bewitched sheep is an exciting one.

Luc Boulanger came over next day. He came on his own two legs. He kept looking uneasily toward the barn.

"Jean LeBlanc," he said, "that sheep with the wooden collar stood in the road and stared at my horse. Now my horse has gone lame."

Jean LeBlanc was sorry about the lame horse. He offered Luc Boulanger the loan of his own horse.

It wasn't long before Luc Boulanger was back again.

"Jean LeBlanc," he said, "you remember how your bewitched sheep nibbled a leaf off my apple tree as she went down the road this morning. Now all the leaves are turning brown and I think the tree will die."

Jean LeBlanc could sympathize with his neighbor about the apple tree. What is as good as an apple baked in pastry or eaten raw in its own red skin?

"I will see that you get some of my apples this summer," he offered.

Everyone told Jean LeBlanc what to do about his sheep. But Jaco Pichet, the butcher, had the best cure for a bewitched sheep.

"Bring her to my place," he said, "and I will butcher her. She will no longer run north and east and south. And I have yet to see the mutton chops that grew any bigger after they left the butcher's scales."

Jean LeBlanc agreed that this was the best thing to do about the sheep with the wooden collar.

He asked Jean-Baptiste to help him get her to the butcher because all the sheep were used to the little boy.

Jean-Baptiste helped his father unfasten the wooden collar from the sheep's neck. He helped tie her hoofs together. He helped lift her into the two-wheeled

cart. And all the time that Jean-Baptiste was helping, he had an unhappy look on his small face.

He sat quietly beside his father on the seat of the cart. His head hung low. He did not ask any questions.

"Bê-e-e," cried the sheep in protest, as the cart rode over a stone in the road.

Jean-Baptiste could not stand himself any longer. "Papa," he said in a low voice, "I have something to tell you."

"Did you forget to close the barn door?" asked his father.

"Worse than that, Papa," said Jean-Baptiste. "The sheep we are taking to the butcher did not go north and get big as a yearling calf. She did not turn east and grow big as a horse. She did not turn south and grow big as a house. She only ran around in the pasture lifting her hoofs and lifting her tail."

Jean LeBlanc pulled on the reins. The horse stopped and the cart stopped.

"Jean-Baptiste," said his father sternly, "you have been telling one big untruth about the poor sheep."

The boy miserably nodded his head. "I don't want her to go to the butcher, Papa," he said. "She never does anything wrong but jump over fences. And she looks so gay when she runs across the pasture lifting her hoofs and lifting her tail."

Jean LeBlanc turned the horse around. The road was not wide so he had to make the horse and cart go back and forth several times before they were headed for home again.

"It is a wicked thing to tell an untruth, Jean-Baptiste," said his father.

The boy nodded some more. Then he fell into deep thought. As usual his deep thought was followed by questions.

"Papa," asked Jean-Baptiste, "is it an untruth when the old heads say that they were chased by the *loup garou*? Was Michel Meloche telling a big untruth when he said that a boat of ghostly fishermen went flying through the clouds?"

Jean LeBlanc suddenly became very busy with his horse. He yelled at her and jerked at the reins as if she were running away.

"My faith, must you spill us into the ditch?" shouted Jean LeBlanc, although his horse wasn't doing anything but jogging along in the middle of the road.

Jean-Baptiste sat waiting for his father's answer.

His father settled back into the seat again. He changed the reins from one hand to the other. He cracked the whip over the horse's back. *Flic, flac.* Then he smiled wisely at his little son.

"The old heads and Michel Meloche do not tell untruths, my little cabbage," he said. "They tell stories."

"What is the difference between an untruth and a story?" asked the boy.

"Ho, ho, there is a great difference," said his father, getting busy with the horse again.

"But what *is* the difference, Papa?" insisted Jean-Baptiste.

The wise look which the boy knew so well crossed

his father's face again.

"The difference is in the way one tells it," said Jean LeBlanc. "When a man tells an untruth, he stands still with his hands in his pockets and his eyes in one place. But when a man tells a story, he waves his arms *ça* and rolls his eyes *ça*. Then all the people know that they can believe it or not—as they wish."

Jean-Baptiste was satisfied with this explanation.

Soon they were home and the boy had to confess to the whole family that he had told an untruth about the sheep with the wooden collar.

Mamma scolded him and the other children were ashamed of him. But Grandmère could understand exactly how it had happened.

She took Jean-Baptiste into her own room and did some more explaining about untruths and stories.

"It is like this, Jean-Baptiste," she said. "You have often heard that when our people first came to Canada, they were surrounded by dangers. There were hostile Indians and fierce animals and new sicknesses. But these dangers were not enough for people as strong and brave as ours. They needed more dangers so they made up *loups garous* and *lutins* and *fi-*

follets. And all the other creatures that only people as smart as ours could think up." Grandmère patted the little boy's head. Then she untied the strings of the round black cap on her head. "But as far as your old Grandmère can see, they are only fancy untruths," she added tartly.

So the sheep had her wooden collar put on her neck again and she went back to the pasture with the others.

Everything was explained to the neighbors in a way which did not shame little Jean-Baptiste. It was done at the Boulangers' stay-awake party one pleasant summer evening. It was a gay fete, with tables full of food and floors full of dancing feet and children.

Old Pierre Boulanger played his violin and even the grandmères danced to that.

When all the feet were tired of dancing and half of the children were asleep, Luc Boulanger waved his hands for quiet.

"A story," he cried. "Who will tell us an exciting story?"

Then Jean LeBlanc rose to his feet and proudly

looked down at his next-to-the-littlest son.

"Jean-Baptiste has a story," he announced. "Only a few have heard it so far, but tonight he will tell it to everyone."

He stood the boy on a chair so everyone could see him. Then he sat down again.

Jean-Baptiste blinked like a little owl pulled out of its tree hole. Then he began to wave his arms *ça* and roll his eyes *ça*.

"We have a strange sheep," he said. "Only last week she did a marvelous thing which I saw with my own eyes. I had gone to the pasture with Toutou, our dog, to bring home the sheep."

Faster waved Jean-Baptiste's arms *ça* and faster rolled his eyes *ça*.

"But the sheep with the wooden collar would not follow the other sheep. She ran away from us. She went north and grew big as a yearling calf. She turned east and grew big as a horse. She turned south and grew big as a house. Then there was a terrible clap of thunder, and lightning flashed all around that great sheep. Fire came out of her eyes and—my faith, I ran home then."

Everyone laughed and clapped. Luc Boulanger

laughed and clapped the loudest. He knew now that the sheep was not really bewitched. Everyone knew that there was nothing wrong with the sheep with

the wooden collar except that she liked to jump over fences.

Luc Boulanger patted Jean-Baptiste on the back. "You are one fine storyteller," he said. "When you get big, you will be as good as old Michel Meloche."